To Amy and Toby, with love R.S.

For my Mum and Dad J.R.

Text copyright © 1994 by Ragnhild Scamell
Illustrations copyright © 1994 by Judith Riches
First published in Great Britain by ABC, All Books for Children,
a division of The All Children's Company Ltd

Library of Congress Cataloging in Publication Data
Scamell, Ragnhild. Rooster crows/by Ragnhild Scamell; illustrated by Judith Riches.
—1st U.S. ed. p. cm. Summary: To prove that the sun rises in the morning because of his crowing,
Rooster bets Bluebird that he can make the sun come up at midnight. [1. Roosters—Fiction. 2.
Pride and vanity—Fiction.] I. Riches, Judith, ill. II. Title. PZ7.S2792Ro 1994 [e]—dc20 93-31348
CIP AC   ISBN 0-688-13290-1 (trade). — ISBN 0-688-13291-X (lib. bdg.)
1 3 5 7 9 10 8 6 4 2
First U.S. edition

The lines from the song "Morning Has Broken," copyright Eleanor Farjeon.
Reprinted by permission of David Higham from *The Christmas Bells*,
published by Oxford University Press.

Rooster Crows

RAGNHILD SCAMELL pictures by JUDITH RICHES

Tambourine Books  New York

"I'm the smartest bird of all," boasted Rooster one morning. "I make the sun rise every day."

"No you don't," said Bluebird. "The dawn chorus of birds does. I sing with them, so I should know.

"Morning has broken, like the first morning..." she trilled.

"Don't start all that noisy business," said Owl, who slept most of the day in the hollow of a tree with Bat.

"You wouldn't like it if the sun didn't rise," said Rooster.

"Oh, yes I would. I'd like it to be night all day," said Owl.

"Me, too," squealed Bat, who was hanging upside down,
listening. "Owl and I could hunt and play and never sleep."
"Well, maybe I won't bother tomorrow morning," said
Rooster.
"It wouldn't make any difference," said Bluebird.

Rooster was furious. He hopped from one leg to another and puffed up his feathers. "I bet you that I could make the sun rise at *midnight* if I tried," he crowed.

"Okay," said Bluebird. "We'll meet here by the old tree at midnight. Owl and Bat can be witnesses."

"No problem," said Rooster and strutted off.

At five minutes to midnight, the tree was full. Owl, Bat, and the entire dawn chorus were there, and Rooster's whole family had come to bring him luck.

"Right," said Owl. "On the last stroke of twelve, Rooster will make the sun rise!"

Rooster preened himself as the town clock
began to strike.

"One ... two ... three ..." hooted Owl.

Rooster stuck out his chest.

"Four ... five ... six ... seven ..."

Rooster plucked out a stray feather.
"Eight ... nine ... ten ... eleven ..."

Rooster pointed his yellow beak at the moon.

"Twelve!"

"COCK-A-DOODLE-DOO! COCK-A-DOODLE-DOO!"

The stars flickered...

but the sun didn't rise.

"COCK-A-DOODLE-DOO!"

crowed Rooster again.

A dark cloud passed in front of the moon.
Everyone shivered and waited.
Finally, after a very long time, Rooster
tried one last desperate crow.

"COCK-A-DOODLE-DOO!"

A bright star shot across the sky
and fell into the night.
"Now look what you've done," said Bat.
"No, no, it's a shooting star," said Owl.
"Make a wish!"

Everybody closed their eyes and wished. Rooster
wished he hadn't boasted so much. Bluebird
wished she hadn't teased Rooster so much.

Slowly and softly, then faster and louder,
Rooster began to crow. The dawn chorus
joined in.

Together, they made the sun rise, just as
it always did.